The Covid Monitor

An Art Is Life Project

London woke up out of bed and ran to her parent's bedroom both excited and nervous at the same time. Excited because she'll finally get to see her friends and teachers after nearly a year. Nervous because she knew that school would be much different than before. But London had plans to ensure that everyone follows the covid safety rules at school.

"Mommy, daddy wake up!" London shouted as she jumped up and down on her parent's king size bed. "It's the first day of school!" She cried.

"London, it's only 5 o'clock and school doesn't start until 8 o'clock." Mom said as she rubbed her eyes with the fist of her hand.

"Yeah honey go back to bed, mom will come and wake you up when it's time for school," dad said.

Mom picked London up and carried her back to her bedroom.

"But mom you don't understand, today I need extra time to get ready!" Cried London.

"Why is that?" Mom asked.

"Because I have to write down the Covid safety rules for everyone at my school to make sure that everybody stays safe." London rambled.

"London, your school already has Covid-19 safety measures in place," Mom explained.

"Yeah but I bet you they don't have a Covid safety monitor!" London said cheerfully.

"What's a Covid safety monitor?" Mom asked.

monitor
covid

"A Covid safety monitor is a person that makes sure that everyone wears their mask and stay at the very least, six feet apart." Explained London.

"I see." Mom replied as she attempts to leave London's room after tucking her in.

"Wait there's more!!!!" London shouted with a pool of excitement.

SOCIAL DISTANCING
2 meters / 6 Feet
2 meters / 6 Feet
WELCOME BACK TO SCHOOL
Washing Hands
2 m
Social Distancing
Don't Touch
Avoid Manny People
NEW NORMAL
SOCIAL DISTANCING
6 ft

"The Covid monitor will be in charge of making sure that everyone keeps their hands clean, that means washing your hands for at least 20 seconds and using hand sanitizer throughout the day to help stop the spread of Covid-19." London explained.

PLEASE, WASH YOUR HANDS
FOR AT LEAST 20 SECONDS

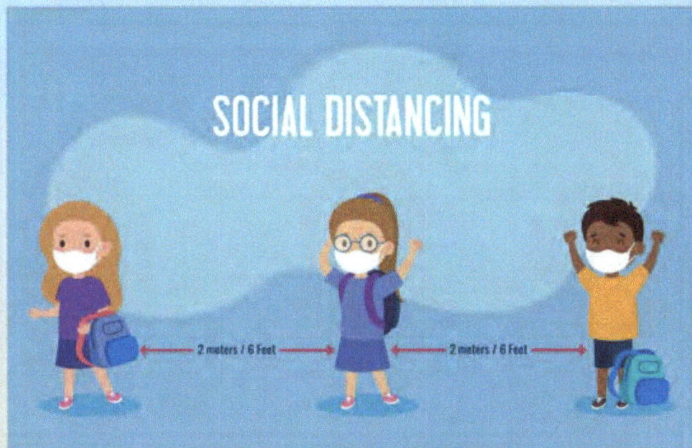

SOCIAL DISTANCING
2 meters / 6 Feet
2 meters / 6 Feet

"Ok London so how often should we wash our hands?" Asked a curious mom.

"Good question." Replied London. "Let me break it down to you," said London. Students and staff should wash their hands;"

- After touching their face

- After using the rest room

- After blowing their nose

- Before and after eating

- After sneezing or coughing

"If soap is not available then you should use hand sanitizer," explained London.

PLEASE, WASH YOUR HANDS
FOR AT LEAST 20 SECONDS
SOCIAL DISTANCING
2 meters / 6 Feet
2 meters / 6 Feet
covid
monitor

"And anyone that's caught breaking the Covid safety rules will have to go to the Covid detention room where they will watch educational videos on how to keep safe during the pandemic." Said London.

"I see." Mom replied.

SOCIAL DISTANCING
2 meters / 6 feet
2 meters / 6 feet
COVID DETENTION
covid
monitor

"Do you know what my educational videos will teach?" Asked London eager to tell.

"I sure do." Mom replied.

"GREAT!!!!" Shouted London while holding both of her arms out in excitement. "My videos will explain why it is important to stay six feet apart," explained London.

"And why is that important?" Asked a curious mom.

6FT APART

"I'm glad you asked," replied London. "Staying six feet apart is important because you never know who's sick." London explained passionately. "some people are asys -asysto- asystomanic." London explained.

"What am I going to do with you London?" Mom asked as she laughed out loud. "The word you are trying to pronounce is called asymptomatic, silly." Mom explained.

ASYMPTOMATIC

"Sorry for getting the name wrong." An embarrassed London replied.

"No worries," said mom. "That's a pretty hard word to pronounce." Mom explained.

"Okay, back to staying six feet apart," that's important because if someone coughs or sneezes on you and they have Covid you can catch it too."

"And don't forget that people who are asymptomatic have little to no symptoms at all." Mom added while yawning.

"I know this school year is going to be hard because me and my friends won't be able to play tag or give each other a hug or a high five, but what keeps my spirits up is knowing that this change is only for a little while. As long as everyone follows the rules things will be back to normal in no time."

FOLLOW THE RULES

"Sounds like you're going to be a great Covid monitor," said mom with a huge smile on her face.

"I'm so proud of you Lunny Poo." Mom gives London a big hug.

"Thanks mom I'm Proud of me too." London falls fast asleep as soon as her mom gives her a kiss on the cheek.

Follow the rules so we can get back to normal

THE END

www.ingramcontent.com/pod-product-compliance
Lightning Source LLC
Chambersburg PA
CBHW042120110726
48006CB00002B/708